MISSING!

Flame

Have you seen this kitten?

Flame is a magic kitten of royal blood, missing from his own world.
His uncle, Ebony, is very keen that he is found quickly.
Flame may be hard to spot as he often appears in a
variety of fluffy kitten colours but you can recognize him
by his big emerald eyes and whiskers that crackle with magic!

He is believed to be looking for a young friend to take care of him.

Could it be you?

If you find this very special kitten please let Ebony,
ruler of the Lion Throne, know.

Sue Bentley's books for children often include animals or fairies. She lives in Northampton and enjoys reading, going to the cinema, and sitting watching the frogs and newts in her garden pond. If she hadn't been a writer she would probably have been a skydiver or brain surgeon. The main reason she writes is that she can drink pots and pots of tea while she's typing. She has met and owned many cats and each one has brought a special sort of magic to her life.

A
Christmas
Surprise

SUE BENTLEY

Illustrated by Angela Swan

PUFFIN

To Tibby, my fondly remembered marmalade sweetie

PUFFIN BOOKS

Published by the Penguin Group
Penguin Books Ltd, 80 Strand, London WC2R ORL, England
Penguin Group (USA) Inc., 375 Hudson Street, New York, New York 10014, USA
Penguin Group (Canada), 90 Eglinton Avenue East, Suite 700, Toronto, Ontario, Canada M4P 2Y3
(a division of Pearson Penguin Canada Inc.)
Penguin Ireland, 25 St Stephen's Green, Dublin 2, Ireland (a division of Penguin Books Ltd)
Penguin Group (Australia), 250 Camberwell Road, Camberwell, Victoria 3124, Australia
(a division of Pearson Australia Group Pty Ltd)
Penguin Books India Pvt Ltd, 11 Community Centre, Panchsheel Park,
New Delhi – 110 017, India
Penguin Group (NZ), 67 Apollo Drive, Rosedale, North Shore 0632, New Zealand
(a division of Pearson New Zealand Ltd)
Penguin Books (South Africa) (Pty) Ltd, 24 Sturdee Avenue, Rosebank,
Johannesburg 2196, South Africa

Penguin Books Ltd, Registered Offices: 80 Strand, London WC2R ORL, England

puffinbooks.com

First published 2007
2

Text copyright © Sue Bentley, 2007
Illustrations copyright © Angela Swan, 2007
All rights reserved

The moral right of the author and illustrator has been asserted

Set in Bembo by Palimpsest Book Production Limited, Grangemouth, Stirlingshire
Made and printed in England by Clays Ltd, St Ives plc

British Library Cataloguing in Publication Data
A CIP catalogue record for this book is available from the British Library

ISBN: 978-0-141-32323-7

Prologue

Dust swirled round the young white lion's paws as he bounded through the dry valley. Flame knew he shouldn't risk being out in the open. But maybe this time it would be safe.

Suddenly, a terrifying roar rang out and an enormous black adult lion burst out from behind some thorn trees and bounded towards him.

'Ebony!'

Flame leapt into a clump of tall grass.
A bright white flash filled the air and
where he had once stood, now
crouched a tiny, snowy-white kitten
with a fluffy tail.

Flame's heart thudded in his tiny
chest as he edged slowly backwards to
where the grass grew more thickly. His
Uncle Ebony was very close. He hoped
this disguise would protect him.

The stems to one side of Flame
parted with a rustle and a big dark
shape pushed towards him. Flame tensed
ready to fight, his emerald eyes sparking
with anger and fear.

'Stay there, Prince Flame. I will
protect you,' growled a deep but
gentle voice.

Flame gave a faint mew of relief, as an old grey lion peered down at him. 'Cirrus. I am glad to see you again. I had hoped that by now, Ebony would be ready to give back the throne he stole from me.'

Cirrus shook his head gravely. 'That will never happen. Your uncle is determined to rule in your place and sends many spies to search for you and kill you. It is not safe for you to be here. Use this disguise and go back to the other world to hide.'

The tiny kitten bared his sharp teeth as he looked up into Cirrus's tired old face. 'I wish I could fight him now!'

Cirrus's eyes flickered with affection. He reached out a huge paw and gently patted Flame's tiny fluffy white head.

'Bravely said, but now is not the time. Return when you are strong and wise.'

Suddenly another mighty roar rang out. The ground shook as huge paws thundered into the tall grass and then came the cracking of crushed stems.

'You cannot hide from me!' roared Ebony's harsh cruel voice.

'Save yourself, Flame! Go quickly!' Cirrus urged.

Sparks glowed in the tiny kitten's silky white fur. Flame mewed softly as he felt the power building inside him. He felt himself falling. Falling . . .

Chapter
ONE

'I really hope it's going to be a white Christmas!' Molly Paget said, peering hopefully out of the landing window. She sighed as raindrops snaked down the glass and blurred her view of the street outside. 'Oh, well. There's still a week to go.'

Molly jumped down the stairs two at a time and went into the kitchen where a delicious spicy smell filled the air. Her mum was just fetching a tray of mince pies out of the oven.

Mrs Paget looked up and smiled. 'I heard you clumping down the stairs. What's the hurry?'

Molly grinned. 'There isn't one. I'm just feeling in a good mood. Can I have one of those pies?'

Her mum nodded. 'Course you can. Take one of those on the plate, they're cooler.'

Molly picked up a mince pie and bit into the sweet crumbly pastry. 'Mmm, yummy. Tastes Christmassy!'

Her mum smiled. 'I'm glad it passes the Molly test!'

'When are Gran and Gramps arriving?' Molly asked, munching.

Her grandparents lived near the coast. She hadn't seen them since the summer holidays, but they were going to spend Christmas at Molly's house. Molly's eyebrows dipped in a small frown as she remembered how during the last visit to her grandparents' house, she had had to take her shoes off before going into the sitting room. Everyone always sat at the table to eat and no one was allowed to watch TV in the daytime. Molly hoped Gran would be less strict this Christmas.

'They'll be here the day before Christmas Eve,' her mum said, wiping her hands on her apron. 'I've still got puddings to make, a cake to ice and heaps of presents to buy. And we haven't even made a start on clearing out the spare bedroom.' A worried look crossed her face. 'Your gran's lovely, but she has very high standards.'

Tell me about it, Molly thought. 'I'll help you. I'm brilliant at clearing up and stuff,' she said brightly.

'It's nice of you to offer, but Molly and the word "help" can sometimes spell trouble!' Mrs Paget said wryly, ruffling her daughter's blonde hair. 'I'll get your dad to give me a hand with the bedroom. It's his parents who are staying, after all.'

'Did I hear my name mentioned?' Mr Paget said, coming into the kitchen. His hair was speckled with dust and there were cobwebs sticking to his blue jumper. He quickly washed his hands before helping himself to a mince pie.

'Da-ad! You've got yucky stuff all over you,' Molly said, laughing. She reached up to pick off a cobweb.

'Have I? I didn't notice,' Mr Paget said around a mouthful of pie. 'I've just been in the attic. I had to move a

mountain of old rubbish to get to the
Christmas tree and decorations. Anyway,
I found them in the end. They're in the
sitting room.'

'Brilliant!' Molly said excitedly, already
speeding out of the kitchen. 'I'm going
to put the tree up right now!'

'Slow down a bit, Molly!' her mum
called after her.

But Molly had already gone. Mr
Paget shook his head slowly. 'Molly's
only got two speeds. Fast and faster!' he
said as he followed his daughter.

By the time her dad came into the
sitting room, Molly had her arms full of
folded, green spiky branches. 'There's an
awful lot of tree,' she said peering into
the long box. 'I don't remember it
being so huge.'

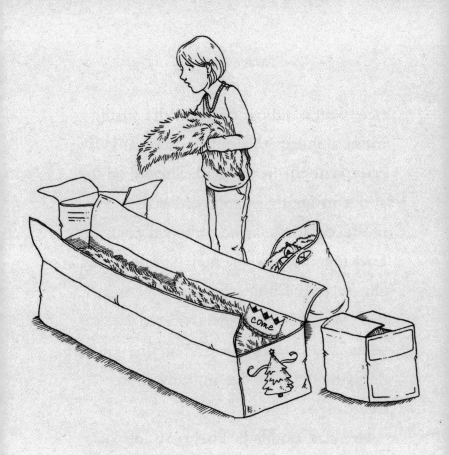

Mr Paget laughed. 'Well it can't have grown since last year, can it, you muppet? I'll fetch the step-ladder.'

'That's a job well done!' Mr Paget said an hour later.

Molly looked up at the Christmas

tree, which almost touched the sitting-room ceiling. 'It's dead impressive. I can't wait to decorate it!' She fished about in another cardboard box and produced some tissue-wrapped packages. Unwrapping one of them, she looked closely at the blue glass bauble. 'Isn't this lovely? It's got silver-frosted snowflake patterns all over it,' she said delightedly. 'Have we got any more like this?'

Her dad nodded. 'There are lots of them. I remember them hanging on our Christmas tree when I was little.'

'Really? They must be ancient then,' Molly said.

'Cheeky!' Mr Paget said, grinning, giving her a playful nudge in the arm. 'I'd forgotten we had those baubles. Be very careful with them, won't you?'

'I will,' Molly promised, unpacking the precious baubles very gently.

Mr Paget peered into the empty cardboard box. 'That's funny. I thought the tinsel and other stuff was in there too. Maybe it's in the garage. I'll go and have a look.'

Molly frowned. She knew that her dad couldn't resist tidying up when he was looking for things. He was bound to be ages. 'Aw, do you have to do it now, Dad?'

Mr Paget grinned at the look on her face. 'Impatient to get going, aren't you? Why don't you make a start on the bottom branches? But you'd better wait for me to come back before you do the ones higher up.'

'OK!' Molly said, already tearing open a packet of little green plastic hooks.

As soon as he'd gone she began hanging baubles on the tree. Soon, the bottom branches were finished. Molly stood back to admire the

way the blue, red and gold glass
gleamed prettily against the dark
green.

Her dad still hadn't come back.
Molly looked longingly up at the
higher branches. She shifted her feet
impatiently. 'Come on, Dad, you
slowcoach,' she grumbled. She hesitated
for a moment longer and then
dragged the step-ladder closer to
the tree.

He was bound to be back in a
minute. She'd just start doing a few
more branches. Climbing halfway up
the ladder, she began fixing baubles to
the branches that were within easy
reach.

This is easy, she thought, *I don't know
what Dad was worrying about.*

She climbed higher to hang more decorations. At this rate, she'd soon have the whole tree finished. At the top of the ladder, Molly leaned out further to try and reach a branch near the top of the tree that would look perfect with the bauble she was holding.

And then she felt the ladder wobble.

'Oops!' Throwing out her arms, Molly tried to grab something to steady herself, but her fingers closed on thin air. She lost her balance and banged against the tree. It shook wildly and decorations began pinging off in all directions.

Molly heard the precious baubles smash into tiny pieces as they hit the carpet. 'Oh, no!' she wailed.

She looked down as she swayed sideways and then everything seemed to happen at once. The ladder and tree both tipped sideways and started to fall to the ground.

'He-elp!' Molly croaked, tensing her whole body for the painful bruising thud as she hit the carpet.

Suddenly, the room filled with a dazzling white flash and a shower of silver sparks. Molly felt a strange warm tingling sensation down her spine as she fell. The air whistled past her ears. There was a sudden jolt, but no hard landing.

To her complete shock, Molly was hovering in mid-air half a metre above the carpet. Swirling all around her was

a snowstorm of brightly sparkling
glitter!

She gasped as she felt herself turning
and then drifting gently down to the
carpet where she landed on her behind
with barely a bump. The sparkling
glitter fizzled like a firework and then
disappeared.

Molly sat up shakily and looked around.

The ladder was upright and the tree was straight and tall once again. The delicate glass baubles were all unbroken and hanging back in place on the branches.

'But . . . I heard them smash! I don't get it . . .' Molly said to herself. What had just happened? She felt like pinching herself to see if she was dreaming.

'I hope you are not hurt?' mewed a strange little voice.

Molly almost jumped out of her skin. 'Who said that?' She twisted round, her eyes searching the room.

Crouching beneath the Christmas tree, Molly saw a tiny fluffy snow-white kitten. Its silky fur seemed to glitter with a thousand tiny, diamond-bright sparkles and it had the biggest emerald eyes she had ever seen.

Chapter
TWO

Molly's eyes widened. She must be more confused and shaken up by her fall than she'd thought. She'd just imagined that the kitten had spoken to her!

She looked at the kitten again and now its silky white fur and bushy tail looked normal. Perhaps it had wandered in when her dad left the door open on his way to the garage. 'Hello. Where've you come from?' she said, kneeling up and reaching a hand towards it.

'I come from far away,' the kitten mewed. 'When I saw you fall I used my magic to save you. I am sorry if I startled you.'

Molly gasped and pulled her hand back as if she had been burned. 'You . . . you can talk!' she stammered.

The kitten blinked up at her with wide green eyes. Despite its tiny size, it didn't seem to be too afraid of her. 'Yes. My name is Prince Flame. What is yours?'

'Molly. Molly Paget,' Molly said. Her mind was still whirling and she couldn't seem to take this all in. But she didn't want to scare this amazing kitten away,

so she sat back on her heels and tried
to stay as small as possible. 'Um . . . I
don't know how you did it, but thanks
for helping me. I could have hurt
myself badly.'

'You are welcome,' Flame purred and
his tiny kitten face took on a serious
look. 'Can you help me, Molly? I need
somewhere to hide.'

'Why do you need to do that?'
Molly asked.

Flame's emerald eyes lit up with
anger. 'I am heir to the Lion Throne.
My uncle Ebony has stolen it and
rules in my place. He wants to keep
my throne, so he sends his spies to
find me.'

'*Lion* Throne?' Molly said doubtfully,
looking at the tiny kitten in front
of her.

Flame didn't answer. He backed
away from the Christmas tree and
before Molly knew what was
happening she was blinded by another
bright silver flash. For a moment she
couldn't see anything. But when her
sight cleared, the kitten had gone and
in its place a magnificent young white

lion stood proudly on the carpet.

Molly gasped, scrambling backwards
on her hands and knees. 'Flame?'

'Yes, it is me, Molly,' Flame replied in
a deep velvety roar.

Molly gulped, just getting used to
the great majestic lion, when there was
a final flash of dazzling light and
Flame reappeared as a silky white
kitten.

'Wow! I believe you,' she whispered.
'That's a cool disguise. No one would
ever know you're a prince!'

Flame pricked his tiny ears and
started to tremble. 'My uncle's spies will
recognize me if they find me. Will you
hide me, please?'

Molly reached out and stroked
Flame's soft little head. He was so tiny

and helpless-looking. Her soft heart melted. 'Of course I will. You can live with me. It'll be great having you to cheer me up if Gran gets in one of her grumpy moods. I bet you're hungry, aren't you? Let's go and find you some food.'

Flame gave an eager little mew.

'Find who some food?' said her dad, coming into the room with a big cardboard box in his arms.

Molly jumped up at once and turned to face him. 'Dad! Something amazing has just happened. I almost fell off the ladder . . . I mean . . . er . . .' she stopped guiltily, deciding that it might be wise to skip that bit. 'I've just found the most amazing kitten and I'm going to look after him. And guess what, he's magic and he can ta–' she stopped suddenly again as Flame gave a piercing howl.

'Flame? What's wrong?' Molly said, crouching down to talk to him.

Flame blinked at her and then sat down on the rug and began calmly washing himself in silence. Molly

looked at him in puzzlement. Why
didn't he explain?

'You and your imagination, Molly
Paget! A talking kitten indeed!' Her dad
shook his head slowly. 'I don't know
where that little kitten came from,
but you'd best pop outside and see if
one of the neighbours is looking for
him!'

'No, they won't be . . .' Molly started
to say, but she saw Flame raise a tiny
paw and put it to his mouth, warning
her to keep quiet. 'I'll go check on the
neighbours,' she finished hastily. She
picked Flame up and went into the
front garden. 'What was all that about,
back there?' she asked him once they
were alone.

'I did not have time to explain

before your father came in that you cannot tell anyone my secret,' Flame mewed softly. 'You must promise, Molly.'

'Oh, no!' Molly's hands flew to her mouth. 'But I almost told Dad everything. Have I already put you in danger?'

Flame shook his head. 'No, it is all right. He did not believe you. Luckily, grown-up humans seem to find it difficult to believe in magic.'

Molly breathed a huge sigh of relief as she looked into Flame's serious little face. 'I promise I'll keep your secret from now on. Cross my heart and hope to die.'

Flame nodded, blinking at her happily.

'I guess we should go and pretend

to look for your owner. Come on,'
Molly urged.

'So we'll just have to keep Flame . . .'
Molly finished explaining as she faced
her mum half an hour later. Flame
nestled in her arms, purring contentedly.

Mrs Paget was stacking things in the
dishwasher. She stood up and reached
out to stroke Flame's soft little white
ears. 'Oh, dear, we hadn't planned on
having a kitten, especially with the
grandparents coming to stay. But if
you've asked all around . . .' she said
uncertainly.

'Oh, I did. I went to *dozens* of houses
and no one knew anything about a
white kitten,' Molly fibbed. 'So – can I
open a tin of tuna for Flame?'

Her mum smiled. 'Go on then. He's really gorgeous, isn't he? And I like his name. But I think that you might have to keep Flame in your bedroom while your gran's here.'

Molly frowned. 'Why? What's she got against kittens?'

Mrs Paget smiled. 'It's not just kittens, it's pets in general. She won't tolerate hairs on the furniture. As for muddy paw prints, wet fur, fleas – shall I go on?'

'Flame hasn't got fleas!' Molly exclaimed. 'Anyway, once Gran meets him I bet even she's bound to love him too. He's the cutest kitten there ever was.'

'I agree with you. But I wouldn't be too sure that your gran will,' her mum warned gently.

Molly hardly heard her. 'Come on, Flame, let's go and tell Dad that Mum says you can stay.' Flame looked up at her and gave an extra loud purr.

Chapter
THREE

'It's the last day of term, so we'll be just
doing fun stuff at school instead of
proper lessons,' Molly said to Flame as
she pulled on her coat a couple of
days later.

Flame had followed her into the hall,
his fluffy white paws padding on the
carpet.

'I have to hurry and catch the bus

now, so I'll see you later,' Molly said, bending down to stroke him. 'I really love having you living here and I wish you could come with me, but we aren't allowed to bring pets to school.'

'But I can come!' Flame told her with a happy little mew. 'I will use my magic to make myself invisible. Only you will be able to see and hear me.'

'Really? That's *so* cool!' Molly said
delightedly. 'OK then. Quick, can you
get into my school bag before Mum
and Dad see you and say you can't
come with me?'

Flame nodded and jumped inside.

It was a short bus ride to school.
Molly put her bag on her lap, so
Flame could poke out his head and
look at the brightly decorated shops
and the big Christmas tree in the
town square. Fairy lights glinted in
the trees lining the streets and more
coloured lights were strung outside
the big stores.

Flame's green eyes grew round with
wonder. 'I have never seen so many
bright lights. They are like glow-worms
in long grass,' he mewed.

'It's because of Christmas,' Molly explained in a whisper. 'The shops are full of presents and stuff and special treats.'

Flame put his head on one side. 'What is Christmas?'

'Oh, I forgot. I don't suppose you have that in your world, do you?' Molly said. 'Christmas is a special time, when all the family gets together to celebrate the baby Jesus being born. We sing carols and give each other presents and eat loads of delicious food until we feel like bursting.' She grinned. 'And we pull things called crackers that go *Bang*! Dad loves the awful jokes you get in them and he always wears his silly paper hat all afternoon!'

Flame looked a bit confused. 'It

sounds very strange, but I think I will like Christmas.'

Molly smiled. She decided to buy him a really special present and put it under the tree for him to unwrap on Christmas morning.

The bus stopped outside the school. Molly got off and shouldered her bag as she walked towards the school gate. A slim, pretty girl with long blonde hair came running up. It was Shona Lamb, one of the most popular girls in Molly's class.

'Hey, Molly!'

'Hi, Shona!' Molly replied. She noticed that Shona was wearing some fabulous new boots. 'Wow! When did you get those?' she asked admiringly. The boots were like the ones Molly

wanted for Christmas, only more
expensive-looking.

Shona glanced down at her smart
boots. 'What? Oh, yesterday. I'd
forgotten about them already. But listen,
I am *so* excited! I bet you can't guess
what Mum's going to buy me for
Christmas!'

Molly pretended to think hard. 'A sports car, a trip round the world, your own private plane?' she joked.

'Very funny. You're a riot!' Shona said, rolling her eyes. 'It's a pony! I'm starting riding lessons soon. You'll be able to come over and watch me riding my very own pony!'

'Um . . . yes,' Molly murmured, imagining Shona prancing about and showing off. *Just what I'd love to do. Not!* she thought.

Shona flicked her long blonde hair over her shoulder and turned to another girl. 'Hi, Jane! You'll never guess what I'm having −'

'As if we care!' whispered a disgusted voice at Molly's side as Shona and the other girl walked away together.

Molly turned and grinned at her best friend. 'Hi, Narinder.'

Narinder Kumar had an oval face and big dark eyes. Her shiny black plait reached to her waist and her brows were drawn together in a frown. 'Sorry, but I can't stand Shona Lamb. She's so spoilt!'

'She can be a bit of a pain,' Molly agreed. 'But I don't mind her. Listen, there's the bell.'

In the classroom, Molly opened her school bag so Flame could jump out. He gave himself a shake and then began washing. Molly knew that Flame was only visible to her, but she couldn't help looking around nervously. When no one seemed to pay Flame any attention, though, she relaxed.

The teacher took the register. Everyone answered as their names were called. '. . . Molly Paget,' called Miss Garret.

There was no reply.

'Molly?' Miss Garret said again.

Narinder nudged Molly. 'Miss Garret's calling your name out.'

Molly did a double take. She had been watching Flame leap from desk to desk, his bushy white tail streaming out behind him. 'Sorry! Here, Miss!' she shouted.

'Thank you, Molly,' Miss Garret said patiently. She finished the register and put it away before speaking to the class. 'Now, everyone, we won't be doing any schoolwork today. We're all going to watch the younger children performing their Christmas play in an hour's time, so we've just time for a quick tidy-up.'

When Molly, Narinder and everyone else groaned Miss Garret smiled. 'Cheer up! It won't take long. Abi and Heather, would you tidy the bookshelves . . .' she began giving out jobs to all the class, '. . . and Molly and Narinder, perhaps you could sort out the art stuff, please?'

'OK, Miss!' Molly jumped up helpfully.

In the storeroom, she and Narinder tidied paper, paints and brushes. Molly spotted a big spray can of fake snow on a high shelf. 'Hey, look at this. It's given me a great idea.'

'What are you going to do?' Narinder asked.

'Wait and see!' Molly slipped the can under her school jumper.

While Narinder was putting the last few things away, Molly wandered across to the window where Flame was curled up.

'What is that? Is it something nice to eat?' the tiny kitten mewed eagerly.

'No, it's fake snow,' Molly whispered.

'I'm going to spray snowflakes on the window as a surprise for everyone.'

Flame blinked at her. 'What is snow?'

Molly looked at him in surprise – maybe it didn't snow where Flame came from. 'It has to get very cold and then rain freezes in pretty patterns and white snowflakes float down from the sky. It's

so beautiful,' she explained. 'I'm really hoping for a white Christmas.'

Flame's emerald eyes widened in astonishment. 'Snow comes from the sky? I would like to see it very much.'

'I'll show you what it looks like!' Molly held the can up to the window and gently pressed the button. Nothing happened, so she shook the can hard and then tried again. Just then, someone tapped her on the shoulder.

'Molly, have you –' Shona began.

Molly lifted her finger as she turned round, but a blast of white foam shot out with a loud whooshing sound. 'Oh, heck! The button's stuck!' she gasped, jabbing at the nozzle to free it.

Shona gave a loud shriek as a powerful jet of fake snow shot all over her jumper.

Chapter
FOUR

Molly finally managed to stop the can spraying. She gaped at Shona in horror.

A thick layer of fake snow covered her from her neck to her waist. It was dripping off the ends of her long blonde hair and splatting on to the floor in soggy white blobs.

'Um, sorry . . .' Molly said lamely.

'You stupid idiot!' Shona howled.
'Look at my hair! It's ruined!'

There were muffled giggles from
Narinder and some other girls, but
Molly didn't laugh. She felt terrible.

Miss Garret hurried over and began
mopping up the sticky mess with
handfuls of paper towels. 'Calm down,
Shona, this stuff washes out.' She
turned to Molly. 'Whatever were you
doing, messing about with that
spray can?'

'I was going to make snowflakes on
the windows, but the nozzle got stuck,'
Molly explained.

'Oo-oh, you fibber!' Shona burst out.
'She did it on purpose, Miss! She aimed
right at me and did a big long squirt!
She's just jealous because I've got new

boots *and* I'm having a pony for
Christmas!'

Molly blinked at Shona in disbelief. 'I
couldn't care less about your rotten
boots and your stupid old pony!'

'That's enough, both of you!' Miss
Garret said, frowning. 'I'll speak to you
about this later, Molly. Come to the

cloakroom, Shona. We're going to have to wash your hair and jumper. The rest of you had better go into the hall. The play's about to start.'

Molly hung back as Miss Garret and Shona and most of her classmates filed out. 'Can I help it if the spray can decides to have a wobbler?' she said to Flame.

'It was very bad luck,' Flame mewed sympathetically. 'I am sorry that I could not use my magic to help you.'

'That's OK. I know you couldn't give yourself away,' Molly said.

Narinder ran up, grinning widely. 'That was *so* hilarious! Serves that snooty Shona right. Stick to your story about spraying her accidentally and you'll be OK!'

'But it really was an accident,' Molly protested.

'Yeah, right!' Narinder said. 'I'm going to the loo. See you in the hall.'

'But . . .' Molly gave up. 'Come on, Flame,' she whispered, shrugging. 'I bet you've never seen a school play.' As she went into the corridor, Flame scampered along at her heels.

Molly almost bumped into two older girls who were waiting just outside the classroom. She recognized them as Alice and Jane, two girls from the class above hers. They both lived near Shona and often hung out with her.

Alice was tall and thin and Jane was smaller with glasses.

As Molly went to walk past, Alice

stuck out a skinny leg, so Molly almost tripped over. 'Oops. Sorry. It was an accident,' she sneered.

'Yeah! Like what you did to Shona,' Jane piped up, glaring at Molly through her glasses. 'You'd better watch your back, you little squirt!'

'Whatever!' Molly said, shrugging,

but her heart beat fast as she walked quickly away from the bigger girls.

Molly tried to enjoy the school play. The younger kids were really cute in their angel wings and tinsel halos, but Alice and Jane's threat was still on her mind.

The rest of the day seemed to drag and Molly only managed to eat a tiny bit of her school dinner, even though it was turkey with all the trimmings. The moment the school bell sounded, Molly headed for the cloakroom.

'Come on, Flame, can you quickly jump into my bag again? We don't want to bump into those two mean girls!' she urged.

She said a hurried goodbye to

Narinder at the gate. 'Sorry I'm in such a rush. I've, er . . . got to hurry home today,' she gabbled. 'I'll phone you!'

Narinder looked surprised. 'OK. See you!' she said, waving.

To Molly's relief, the bus was waiting at the bus stop. She managed to jump on to it, just before it pulled away. She reached home safely and was hanging her school bag in the hall when her mum appeared from upstairs.

'Hello, love. You look a bit glum. Is something wrong?' Mrs Paget asked.

'I . . . um, had a bit of an accident,' Molly began. She told her about spraying Shona. 'And everyone thinks I did it on purpose!'

'But of course you didn't!' Mrs Paget said indignantly. 'You sometimes act without thinking first, but you haven't got a mean bone in your body!' She gave Molly a hug. 'Don't worry yourself about it. It'll all be forgotten about by next term.'

'Do you think so?' Molly asked, biting her lip.

'Definitely,' Mrs Paget said firmly. She turned towards the plain white

Christmas cake on the kitchen table.
Icing pens, food colouring and
marzipan lay next to it. 'How would
you like to decorate the cake for me?
I was about to make a start on it, but I
really need to nip out to the shops.'

'Cool!' Molly said, immediately
cheering up. 'Just leave it to me,
Mum!'

As soon as she'd waved goodbye to
her mum, Molly came back into the
kitchen and began making a marzipan
robin. Flame sat on a kitchen chair,
watching in fascination as she put the
robin on the cake and then made
wriggly lines with the icing pens.

Molly looked down at her work so
far. 'Not bad. But it needs something
else,' she said, frowning. 'I know! I'll

make a snowman. I wonder if Mum's got any of that white ready-made icing stuff left.'

Climbing on to a kitchen chair, she peered into the cupboard above the table. She stood up on tiptoe and poked about behind a stack of tins. 'I can't see any –'

'Look out!' Flame mewed warningly as Molly's elbow brushed against the tins.

It was too late. Three heavy tins fell out and landed right on the cake. Thud! The cake broke apart and icing and bits of fruit cake shot all over the table.

'Oh, no!' Molly groaned in dismay.

Flame stood up on his back legs and rested his front paws on the table.

'Do not worry, Molly. I will help you,' he purred.

Molly felt a warm tingling down her spine as bright sparks ignited in Flame's silky white fur and his whiskers crackled with electricity. He lifted a tiny glittering white paw and sent a laser beam of silver sparks towards the ruined cake.

As Molly watched, the sparkling beam moved back and forth, forming the cake back into shape from the bottom up. 'Wow! It's just like watching special effects in a sci-fi movie!' she said delightedly.

The cake was half built up again, when Flame's sparkling ears twitched. 'Someone is coming!' he warned.

A second later, Molly heard the front

door slam and voices echoed in the hall. 'Hello, is anyone in? Surprise, surprise!' called Gran Paget.

'Oh, golly!' Molly gasped in panic, jumping down from the chair. 'What's she doing here? Do something, Flame!'

Chapter
FIVE

Flame's whiskers crackled with another
bright burst of power.

As Molly watched, everything went
into fast forward. The laser beam
whizzed back and forth, re-forming the
cake in treble quick time. Whump!
The cake plonked itself on the plate.
Whoosh! The tins zoomed into the air.
One, two, three – they stacked

themselves in the cupboard. Slam! The cupboard door closed.

Just as the last fizzing spark faded from Flame's white fur, Gran Paget came into the kitchen. Gramps and Molly's dad were with her.

'Gran! Gramps!' Molly cried, hugging them each in turn.

'Hello, love,' Gramps said, kissing her cheek. 'I bet you weren't expecting us, were you? We arranged to come a few days early to do some shopping and sightseeing. Your dad's just picked us up from the train station.'

'I wanted it to be a surprise. I don't know how I managed to keep it a secret,' Mr Paget said, grinning at his daughter.

A small flicker of unease rose in Molly's mind. 'Er. . . Dad? Does Mum know about this?' she whispered to him.

'Not yet. But she's going to be delighted. I can't wait to see the look on her face!' he replied.

Neither can I, Molly thought, remembering the state the spare room was in.

She heard the front door slam. 'I'm back,' called Mrs Paget.

'Uh-oh,' Molly breathed, running out to meet her mum and almost colliding with her. 'Guess who's here! Gran and Gramps!'

Mrs Paget almost jumped out of her skin. She dropped one of her bags and shopping began rolling everywhere. 'Molly! Do you have to dart about like that?' she scolded.

'Oops, sorry!' Molly apologized, picking up the groceries.

Her dad and grandparents came out of the kitchen to help and soon everyone was laughing. Mrs Paget hugged the grandparents. 'What a lovely surprise,' she said, looking hard at her husband.

'Time for a cup of tea and a mince pie!' Mr Paget said hurriedly.

'I'll fill the kettle,' Molly said, rushing back into the kitchen.

Her mum followed her in. As she caught sight of the Christmas cake, she stopped dead. 'Molly? Are you responsible for this?' she exclaimed.

'Um . . . yes. Sorry it didn't turn out very well . . .' Molly said over her shoulder. She was so grateful that Flame had put the cake back together in the nick of time that she had completely forgotten about the lop-sided robin and messy squiggles of icing.

'But it's wonderful!' her mum said. 'What a lovely snow scene, with a robin on a fence, and I love the snow kitten. Clever old you!'

Snow kitten? Molly spun round.

A big grin broke out on her face as
she saw that the cake was even better
than before the cans had fallen on it.
She bent down to look under the table
where Flame was sitting. 'Thanks,
Flame,' she whispered.

Flame winked at her and began
purring loudly. Suddenly he gave a
startled yowl as a pair of arms shot

under the table and grabbed him.

'How did that naughty cat get in?'
Gran scolded. 'You're going outside,
right now! Animals have no place in
kitchens!' Before Molly could react,
she opened the back door, plonked
Flame outside, and shut the door
firmly.

Molly gaped at her. 'But it's cold out
there! And Flame's only a tiny kitten!'
she protested.

'He'll be fine. He's got a nice thick
fur coat to keep him warm,' Gran said,
dusting off her hands.

Molly scowled. She marched across
and opened the back door. 'Flame's
my kitten. If he has to stay outside,
I'm staying with him!' she said
stubbornly.

'Now, Molly. Don't be hasty . . .' her mum warned gently.

'I don't care what anyone says!' Molly fumed. 'I'll stay out here all night if I have to!' She picked Flame up and cradled him against her. She could feel him trembling. 'Flame lives in the house. Tell her, Mum.'

'Calm down, Molly. I expect your gran thought Flame was just a stray who'd got in somehow. She wasn't to know you had a new kitten and I don't suppose your dad thought to tell her,' Mrs Paget said reasonably. She turned to Gran. 'Molly's right. Flame does live in the house. He's a very clean kitten.'

Gran drew herself up. She didn't look pleased. 'Have it your way then, but I'm afraid I don't hold with spoiling pets. They have to learn their place.'

Yes, and Flame's place is with me, Molly thought crossly. She stormed out of the kitchen and hurried up to her bedroom with Flame.

She curled up on her bed and lay there cuddling Flame and feeling miserable. Gran hated Flame. It was unbelievable. How could anyone not love her gorgeous kitten as much as she did?

'It's not fair!' she complained, stroking Flame's fluffy white fur. 'Now you'll have to be shut in my bedroom all the time Gran's here.'

Flame's bright eyes sparked with mischief. 'I do not think so! Remember how I came to school with you. No one knew that I was there, did they?'

A slow, delighted grin spread across Molly's face. Of course, Flame could make himself invisible whenever he wanted to!

Molly woke early the next morning and turned over to stroke Flame who was curled up beside her. *Strange,* she thought, *something seems different.*

'Listen? Can you hear anything?' she said to him.

Flame lifted his head and yawned sleepily. 'I cannot hear anything.'

'Exactly!' Molly cried. She jumped out of bed, threw open the curtains and peered out of the window. 'Oh! It looks so beautiful,' she gasped.

The garden looked as if someone had thrown a thick white blanket all over it. Snow had made bushes and flower beds into soft blurry humps. Everything gleamed brightly under a clear silver sky.

'Hurrah!' Molly did a little dance of happiness. 'It *is* going to be a white Christmas this year! Flame! Come and look. It's been snowing overnight.'

Flame bounded across to the window sill in a single leap. He stared out at the garden with shining eyes. 'Snow is very beautiful,' he purred happily, his warm kitten breath fogging the glass.

'Come on, Flame. I'm going to ask Mum and Dad if we can go sledging in the park!' Molly decided, already

searching for a warm jumper and
old boots.

She found her dad in the sitting
room, finishing his breakfast cup of tea.
'Sledging in the park's a great idea,' he
said when Molly had finished speaking.
'I'd rather come with you, but your
mum's promised to take Gran and
Gramps for a mooch about in the
big stores.'

'Poor you!' Molly said, grinning at
the look on his face. 'Never mind, we
can go sledging another day.'

She was about to go out, when some
new knitted cushions caught her eye.
One had lime green and purple stripes
and the other had orange and blue
checks. 'Wow! Where did those come
from?' she asked.

'They were a present from your
gran. She's mad about knitting,' her dad
said wryly. 'They look . . . um . . .
interesting with our red sofa, don't
they?'

'Well, you can't miss them!' Molly
spluttered with laughter. 'I think I'll
phone Narinder and ask her if she
wants to meet Flame and me at the

park,' she decided when she could speak again. 'Have a nice time shopping, Dad.'

'I'll try to,' he said mournfully. 'See you later. Come back home by lunchtime, love.'

'OK,' Molly answered, skipping into the hall.

Ten minutes later, she was bundled up in a warm coat, scarf and gloves. 'Come on, Flame. Let's go and meet 'Rinder,' she said, opening the front door.

Flame leapt straight out and then gave a mew of surprise as he sank into the snow. He gambolled about, jumping sideways and then he stopped to sniff at the snow. 'It tastes delicious,' he purred happily, nibbling a bit.

Molly laughed as she watched him.

Sometimes it was hard to remember that this cute playful kitten was a majestic lion prince. 'It might be best if you ride on the sledge,' she decided. 'We'll get there faster and your feet will stay warm.'

'My magic will keep me warm,' Flame mewed, but he sprang on to the boat-shaped, red plastic sledge like Molly suggested and settled d own.

Molly set off, dragging her sledge and Flame behind her.

The park was only a couple of minutes away. Lots of kids were already there. Some had sledges and others sat on tin trays or plastic bags as they slid down the snowy slopes. Molly saw Narinder waving as she came

towards her. 'Hi! Isn't this brilliant!'
she cried.

'Yeah! I love snow!' Molly said.

'Hey, I didn't know you had a kitten.
Isn't he absolutely gorgeous! Where did
you get him from?' Narinder said,
bending down to stroke Flame's fuzzy
little head.

Flame purred and rubbed against
Narinder's gloved hand.

'I haven't had him long,' Molly
said quickly, hoping to avoid awkward
questions. 'Come on. Let's go
sledging!'

She and Narinder trudged up the
steep snowy slope with their sledges.
At the top, Molly sat down and Flame
jumped into her lap.

'I'll race you!' Molly said to Narinder.

'You're on!' Narinder shouted back.
'Ready? One. Two. Three!'

'Hold on, Flame! Here we go!' Molly
cried, pushing off with her hands.

Molly and Narinder flew down the
slope, side by side. Flame's silky white
fur blew back in the cold air.

'Whe-ee-e!' Molly yelled, grinning

across at Narinder as her sledge edged forward. 'We're winning!'

Suddenly, near the bottom of the slope, she felt the sledge skidding sideways. The front of it clipped a small bank of snow and it spun round and tipped over. Molly shot into the air and landed in the soft powdery snow with Flame still on her lap.

Narinder whizzed past, yelling triumphantly.

'Next time!' Molly shouted. Giggling, she started to get up. 'Wasn't that brilliant, Flame —'

'Well if it isn't that snotty little squirt who sprayed stuff all over me in class!' said a voice. Shona Lamb stood there with her hands on her hips. She wore a smart pink ski jacket and fluffy ear-muffs. 'Listen to her talking to her kitten. As if it's going to answer her!'

Molly's tummy gave a horrid little lurch as she saw that Shona wasn't alone. Alice and Jane, Shona's mean older friends were with her.

Chapter
SIX

'Now you're for it!' warned Shona,
scooping up a big snowball.

'Yeah!' Jane said, bending down and
making a snowball too.

'Three on one isn't fair!' Molly
said in a wobbly voice as she got to
her feet. She quickly placed Flame on
the sledge out of harm's way. He
stood there, tiny legs planted wide,

his fur and bushy tail bristling with
fury.

'Tough!' Alice said, grinning nastily.

Molly's mouth dried. Flame might
want to help her, but he couldn't use
his magic without giving himself away.
Narinder was at the bottom of the
long slope.

She was on her own.

A snowball hit Molly on the arm, but the powdery snow broke and it didn't really hurt. Another one landed on her back and then one hit her ear with a stinging blow. Molly hardly had time to make a snowball of her own and throw it, before she was hit again.

'Ow!' she cried as another snowball hit her neck and icy snow trickled inside her coat collar. 'That's enough now. You've paid me back,' she said, trying hard not to cry.

'Maybe she's right,' Shona said uncertainly. 'Let's go.'

'No, wait! I haven't finished with her yet!' Jane had a mean hard look on her face. She was patting her gloved hands together, making a snowball into a firm lump. Before Molly realized what she was going to do, Jane drew back her arm and aimed at Flame.

'No!' Molly screamed, throwing herself in front of him. The hard snowball smacked into her cheek with bruising force.

Molly gasped, stunned. Her cheek felt as if it was on fire and she felt sick and dizzy.

'Now you've really hurt her!' Shona said worriedly. 'She's gone all white and shaky!'

Jane and Alice exchanged glances. 'Leg it!' Jane said.

Shona came over to Molly. 'Are you all right? I'm sorry. I didn't mean it to go so far,' she said, biting her lip.

'Just leave me alone,' Molly murmured shakily.

As Shona ran after her friends, Molly's legs gave way and she sank on to the snow. Flame scampered up to her in an instant. 'Quick, Molly. Put me inside your coat,' he mewed urgently.

Molly did so. As soon as Flame was hidden from sight, Molly heard a faint crackling as sparks ignited in his fur and there was a soft glow from inside her coat as Flame's whiskers fizzed with power. The familiar warm tingling spread down her back and Molly felt a gentle prickling in her sore cheek. The pain drained away, just as if she had poured it down the sink.

'That's much better. Thanks, Flame,' she whispered.

Flame touched her chin with his tiny cold nose. 'You saved me from being badly hurt, Molly. You were very brave.'

Molly's heart swelled with a surge of affection for him. 'I'm not really. I just couldn't bear to think of anything happening to you. I love having you for my friend. I hope you can stay with me forever.'

'I will stay for as long as I can,' Flame purred gently.

'Molly! Are you all right?' Narinder's breath puffed out in the cold air as she came panting up the slope. 'I feel awful. I saw those bullies setting on you, but I couldn't get to you quickly enough to help.'

Molly grinned. 'Don't worry about it, 'Rinder, it's hard to run uphill in the

snow. Anyway, I'm OK. And I reckon
they'll leave me alone now they've had
their own back. Come on, let's go back
up. I'm definitely going to beat you to
the bottom this time!'

'Hi, we're home!' Molly sang out as she
dumped her coat and boots and went
towards the sitting room.

Her mum poked her head round the door. 'Shh. Can you be quiet, love? Gran's having forty winks in there. We've just been on a long hunt for some special knitting wool and she's worn out. Did you have a good time in the park?'

'Great, thanks. Where's Dad and Gramps?' Molly asked.

'In the garage, pottering about,' her mum replied. 'They need a bit of light relief after all those shops! Lunch won't be long, so don't go away. It's home-made tomato soup.'

'Sounds nice.' Molly went quietly into the sitting room and sat on the sofa to read a magazine. 'There's no need to become invisible, Flame. Gran's *well* asleep. Listen!' she whispered, giggling.

Soft snores rose from the corner chair, where Gran was asleep with her knitting bag in her lap. As Molly watched, the bag slowly tipped forward and a ball of blue wool fell out and rolled across the carpet.

Flame couldn't resist. He gave a tiny eager mew and pounced on it. Play-growling and lashing his tail, he chased the ball of wool round the back of Gran's chair.

Molly bit back a splutter of laughter as Flame reappeared with the ball of wool held proudly in his mouth. He tossed his head and the trailing wool tightened. Gran's knitting seemed to jump out of the bag. On the end of the trailing wool there was now a half-finished, blue and white striped sock.

'Uh-oh. Now you've really done it!'
Molly breathed. She crept forward to
rescue the knitting. But it was too late.

Gran opened her eyes, yawned and sat
up. As she spotted Flame she gave a
gasp of horror. 'My knitting! You little
menace! What have you done? Just wait
until I get my hands on you!'

Flame laid his ears back and yowled

with panic. He tried to run away, but the wool was wound tightly round his legs, and he fell over his own feet.

Red-faced, Gran got up from the chair but Molly was already bounding across the room. She got to Flame first. 'Stop wriggling,' she scolded gently, untangling him as quickly as she could. 'That's it! You'd better scoot! Gran's on the warpath!'

Flame didn't need telling twice. Flattening his ears, he zoomed out and ran upstairs. Molly picked up the mess of wool and knitting and handed it to Gran.

Gran had a face like thunder. 'That sock's ruined and I don't fancy using the wool again after that little beggar's been chewing it. Those socks were for

your dad. I'll never have them finished
for Christmas now. I told you that
kitten would be nothing but trouble!'

'Sorry, Gran,' Molly said in a subdued
voice. *Why didn't Gran just buy socks, like
normal people did, anyway?* she thought.
'Flame didn't mean to be naughty. He
was just playing.'

'Soup's ready! Molly could you go

and tell your dad and Gramps, please?'
Mrs Paget called from the hall.

'Will do, Mum. Phew!' Molly
breathed gratefully, escaping as quickly
as she could.

Chapter
SEVEN

Molly had Flame in her shoulder bag as she walked out to the car with her dad the following afternoon. It was the day before Christmas Eve and they were all going shopping at the Christmas market in the square.

'I've been meaning to say thank you to you and Flame,' her dad said.

'What for?' Molly asked, puzzled.

'For saving me from having to wear blue and white striped socks!' he said, pulling a face.

Molly laughed and gave him a friendly shove and then her face grew serious. 'Gran was furious about having her knitting spoiled. I don't think she'll ever like Flame now,' she said sadly.

'Oh, you never know. Gran's bark is worse than her bite,' her dad said.

'Really?' Molly said; then seeing her grandparents coming out of the house, she quickly got into the car with Flame.

As her dad drove them all into town, Molly counted out her pocket money. She had been saving it up for weeks and had enough to buy gifts for everyone – including Flame. It was

exciting to think of all the lovely things she was going to buy.

The market was crowded and colourful. It was full of exciting stalls, selling things from all round the world. Coloured light bulbs flashed on the huge Christmas tree and tinsel glittered under the streetlamps. People

wrapped in hats and scarves walked
about carrying bags and mounds of
presents.

As Molly, her parents and
grandparents strolled among the stalls
Flame popped his head out of her
shoulder bag. His nose twitched as he
enjoyed the smells of roasting chestnuts
and hot spiced chocolate.

'Isn't this great?' Molly whispered to
Flame, looking at some pretty silk
scarves. 'I'm going to buy one of these
for Mum.'

Flame didn't answer, but Molly was
too busy to notice. She paused to
listen to some carol singers holding
lanterns, their sweet voices rising on
the frosty air. At other stalls, she
bought lavender bags for Gran, a key

ring for Gramps and a new wallet for
her dad.

'I'm doing really well with buying
presents,' she said, glancing down at
Flame. But his head wasn't sticking up
out of her bag. 'Flame? Are you having
a nap?' She reached her hand inside the
bag to stroke him and her fingers
brushed against a tightly curled up
trembling little body. 'What's wrong?'
she asked in concern.

'My uncle's spies are here. I can
sense them,' Flame whined softly. 'I
must hide!'

Molly's heart clenched with panic.
Flame was in terrible danger. Her mind
raced as she tried to decide what to do.
There was no way she was letting
anyone hurt Flame!

An idea jumped into her mind. 'Don't worry! We're leaving,' she whispered to Flame.

Spotting her parents at a nearby cheese stall, Molly dashed straight over. 'Can we go home?' she pleaded. 'I feel awful. I think I'm going to be sick!'

Gran and Gramps appeared, holding some parcels. 'What's wrong?' asked Gramps.

'It's Molly. She feels ill,' Mr Paget answered.

'It's probably all the free samples she's tried,' Gran said. 'I expect she'll be OK in a minute.'

'No, I won't!' Molly insisted. She felt desperate. Rolling her eyes, she gave a loud groan and clutched her tummy. 'I think I'm dying! It'll be all your fault if I collapse right here in the market.'

Even Gran looked alarmed.

'Don't be so dramatic, Molly. It's only a bit of old tummy ache,' her dad said mildly, but he looked worried. 'Perhaps we'd better take you home.'

'We've almost finished shopping, haven't we? Let's all go back,' Gramps said.

Molly could have kissed him. She flashed him a grateful smile and then remembered that she was supposed to be feeling sick.

As they all hurried towards the car park, she stroked Flame's trembling little form. 'Hang on! We'll soon be out of here,' she whispered.

Molly didn't see the dark shadowy

shapes slipping between the stalls or the narrow cruel eyes that raked the crowded market.

'He is very close,' growled a cold voice.

'Ebony will reward us well for finding the young prince,' hissed the other spy.

'I'm being allowed to stay up late tonight. We're all going to midnight mass at the cathedral. You'll love it!' Molly said happily the following afternoon.

Flame was curled up on her duvet, surrounded by bits of shiny wrapping paper, ribbons and sticky tape. He was back to his normal self, now that the danger from his uncle's spies seemed to be far behind him.

Molly was wrapping her presents in
shiny foil paper. 'I hope those horrible
mean cats keep on going until they
jump into the sea and sink! And then
you can stay with me forever,' she said
to Flame.

Flame blinked up at her. 'They may
come back and then I will have to
leave at once. Do you understand,
Molly?' he mewed seriously.

'Yes,' Molly answered in a small voice.

'But I'm not going to think about that.'

She finished wrapping her presents and putting bows on them. 'I'll go and put them under the tree now,' she said to herself.

Leaving Flame dozing, she went downstairs into the sitting room. Gramps was reading a newspaper and Gran was knitting. She had started a new scarf in pink, brown and yellow stripes.

There was the sound of voices from the kitchen.

'Hi, Gran. Hi, Gramps,' Molly said, bending down to put her presents with the others. A sudden thought struck her. Surely there was one missing. 'Oh, no,' she gasped. 'I've forgotten to buy one for Flame.' In all the urgency of getting

Flame away from his enemies, she'd completely forgotten to get him a present.

'What's that, love?' Gramps asked, looking up from his paper.

Molly told him. '. . . and Flame's going to be the only one without a present to open on Christmas morning,' she finished glumly.

'Oh, that's a shame,' Gran said.

Molly looked at her in surprise. It sounded like she really meant it. 'I'll just have to go to the shops and get one. Maybe Dad will take me. I'll ask him,' she said on her way to the door.

'I think it's too late, dear,' Gramps said. 'The shops all close early on Christmas Eve.'

'Oh, yes,' Molly remembered with

dismay. She stopped and turned back round. This was awful. What was she going to do? Flame would have to go without a present.

Gran looked thoughtful. 'I've got an idea,' she said, producing the scrap of blue and white sock from her knitting bag. 'I reckon I could make this into a toy mouse. I'll only take a few ticks to make some ears and a tail.'

'Do you mean it?' Molly gaped at her gran. Maybe she *did* like Flame a little bit, after all. She flew over and gave her a huge hug. 'That would be perfect! Thanks, Gran. You're the best!'

Chapter
EIGHT

Molly felt full of the magic of
Christmas as she walked into the
cathedral. The ancient walls flickered
with the light of countless candles, and
footsteps echoed on the stone floor.

Even though it was long past Molly's
usual bedtime, she didn't feel a bit tired.

Flame was in her shoulder bag. And it
didn't matter if everyone could see him.

Animals and their owners were all welcome for the special Christmas Eve service.

'Isn't it gorgeous in here?' she whispered to him, looking at the candlelight flickering on the stained-glass windows and the big vases of flowers and holly and ivy.

The church was packed and everyone was in a good mood. There were hot drinks, mince pies and bags of fruit and nuts to nibble. A special band with amazing instruments from all round the world played and dancers performed folk dances. And then the cathedral choir sang and everyone joined in with the carols.

Molly caught sight of Shona with her parents. She hesitated for a moment and then waved at her. Shona looked surprised and then she waved back, smiling. 'Happy Christmas!' she called.

'Happy Christmas!' Molly replied happily.

'I've got my pony. You'll have to come over and see him. He's gorgeous,' Shona said.

Molly bit back a grin. She was glad they were friends again, but Shona would never change.

After the service finished, Molly and Flame, her parents and grandparents all trudged home through the snow. A big silver moon shed its light on to the glittering snow crystals underfoot.

Molly held her bag close to her chest, so that she could stroke Flame without anyone noticing. 'This has to be the best Christmas Eve ever,' she whispered to him.

Just before she went up to bed, Gran pressed a tiny package into her hand. 'For Flame. I hope he likes it,' she said.

Molly threw her arms round her and kissed her cheek. 'I love you, Gran.'

Gran's eyes looked moist and shiny. 'I
love you too, Molly.'

Molly slipped Flame's present under
the tree before she went up to her
bedroom. She felt so excited that she
was sure she wouldn't sleep a wink.
She'd just lie there in the dark, waiting
for Christmas Day.

After undressing and cleaning her
teeth, Molly slipped into bed. 'Good
night, Flame,' she whispered, breathing
in his sweet kitten smell as she
cuddled him.

Seconds later, she was asleep.

It felt like about five minutes later,
when Molly opened her eyes. She was
amazed to find the winter light pushing
through her curtains.

'Come on, Flame. It's Christmas
morning!' She leapt out of bed, threw
her dressing gown on over her
pyjamas and pushed her feet into her
slippers.

She shot down the stairs two at a
time, with Flame gambolling at her
heels.

'Happy Christmas!' she said, bouncing into the sitting room.

Her mum and dad and grandparents were already dressed and sitting with hot drinks. They looked up and smiled as Molly burst in.

'Happy Christmas, love,' said her dad, pouring more coffee.

'Happy Christmas,' chorused her mum and Gran and Gramps.

'Can we open our presents now?' Molly said, going to sit cross-legged on the rug with Flame in her lap.

'We thought you'd never ask!' Gramps said. 'We've all been waiting for you to wake up.'

Molly unwrapped her presents eagerly. She had some books and music and lots of other brilliant stuff.

But best of all were the new boots she'd been hoping for. 'Cool! Thanks so much for my lovely presents, everyone!' she said, putting the boots on straight away.

'Interesting look with those pyjamas!' her dad joked.

Everyone laughed.

'Here's your present, Flame!' Molly loosened the wrapping paper.

He ripped it open with his sharp teeth and claws, a look of delight on his tiny face. The moment Flame saw Gran's knitted mouse, he gave an excited little mew. Grabbing it in his mouth he padded proudly round the room, his bushy tail held in the air.

'I'm glad someone likes my knitting!'

Gran said, giving Molly's dad one of her looks.

Mr Paget kissed Gran's cheek and then winked at Molly.

Molly choked back a laugh. 'Flame adores his mouse, Gran! Um . . . is it OK if I phone Narinder and ask if she wants to come and listen to my new CDs later on?' she asked.

'Course it is,' said her mum. 'And then can you hurry up and get dressed? Breakfast's almost ready. It's your favourite.'

'OK,' Molly said, going out into the hall.

Suddenly, Flame streaked past her and zoomed upstairs so fast that he was a tiny white blur. Molly frowned. He'd never done that before.

'Flame? What –' she broke off as a
horrible suspicion rose in her mind. She
started running after him, her phone
call forgotten for the moment.

As Molly reached the landing, there
was a bright flash from her open
bedroom door. She dashed into her

room. Flame stood there, no longer a tiny kitten, but a magnificent young white lion with a coat that glittered and glinted with a thousand sparkles. An older grey lion with a wise and gentle face stood next to him.

'Prince Flame! We must leave now!' the grey lion growled urgently.

Molly caught her breath as she understood that Flame's enemies had found him again. This time he was going to leave for good.

Flame's emerald eyes crinkled in a fond smile. 'Merry Christmas, Molly. Be well, be strong,' he rumbled in a velvety growl as a whoosh of silver sparks spun round him. And then he and the old lion disappeared.

'Goodbye, Flame. Take care. I'll never

forget you. I hope you regain your throne,' Molly said, her heart aching.

Molly knew that she'd remember this Christmas forever. Having Flame as her friend, even for only a short time, was the best present she would ever have. She stood there for a moment longer as she brushed away a tear.

And then she remembered Narinder. As Molly went downstairs to phone her, she found herself smiling.

Win a Magic Kitten goody bag!

An urgent and secret message has been left for Flame from his own world, where his evil uncle is still hunting for him.

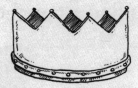

Five words from the message can be found in royal lion crowns hidden in *A Christmas Surprise*.
Find the hidden words and put them together
to complete a special Christmas message.
Send it in to us and we will put every correct message
in a draw and pick out one lucky winner who will receive
a purrfect Magic Kitten gift!

Send your secret message, name and address on a postcard to:
Magic Kitten Competition
Puffin Books
80 Strand
London WC2R 0RL

Hurry, Flame needs your help!

Good luck!

puffin.co.uk

Visit:
penguin.co.uk/static/cs/uk/0/competition/terms.html
for full terms and conditions

A Puzzle of Paws

Flame needs to find a purrfect new friend!

And that's how Rosie's worries about moving house get easier to bear when cuddly black kitten Flame becomes part of the furniture . . .

A Shimmering Splash
Flame needs to find a purrfect new friend!

And that's how the sun suddenly shines on Lorna's gloomy island stay when playful amber and white kitten Flame comes ashore . . .

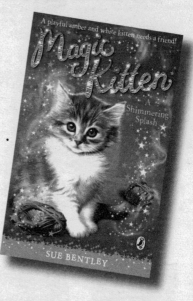

A Summer Spell
978–0–141–32014–4

Classroom Chaos
978–0–141–32015–1

Double Trouble
978–0–141–32017–5

Star Dreams
978–0–141–32016–8

Moonlight Mischief
978–0–141–32153–0

Sparkling Steps
978–0–141–32155–4

Seaside Mystery
978–0–141–32198–1

A Circus Wish
978–0–141–32154–7

A Glittering Gallop
978–0–141–32156–1

Firelight Friends
978–0–141–32199–8

A Shimmering Splash
978–0–141–32200–1

A Puzzle of Paws
978–0–141–32201–8

A Christmas Surprise
978–0–141–32323–7

puffin.co.uk

Coming Soon . . .

Picture Perfect	A Splash of Forever
978–0–141–32348–0	978–0–141–32349–7

puffin.co.uk